Tiny Tales

Fiction From Kent

First published in Great Britain in 2007 by
Young Writers, Remus House, Coltsfoot Drive,
Peterborough, PE2 9JX
Tel (01733) 890066 Fax (01733) 313524
All Rights Reserved

© Copyright Contributors 2007
SB ISBN 978-1-84431-360-0

Disclaimer
Young Writers has maintained every effort
to publish stories that will not cause offence.
Any stories, events or activities relating to individuals
should be read as fictional pieces and not construed
as real-life character portrayal.

Foreword

Young Writers was established in 1991, with the aim of encouraging the children and young adults of today to think and write creatively. Our latest primary school competition, *Tiny Tales*, posed an exciting challenge for these young authors: to write, in no more than fifty words, a story encompassing a beginning, a middle and an end. We call this the mini saga.

Tiny Tales Fiction From Kent is our latest offering from the wealth of young talent that has mastered this incredibly challenging form. With such an abundance of imagination, humour and ability evident in such a wide variety of stories, these young writers cannot fail to enthral and excite with every tale.

Contents

Sophie Phillips (9) 13

Bligh Junior School
Hannah Aldous (11) 14
Rebecca Peard (11) 15
Kelly Greenfield 16

Churchill CE Primary School
Ben Carter (10) 17
Emma Fitch (11) 18
Harry Bond (11) 19
Bethany Taylor (11) 20
Baldeep Chahal (10) 21
Gabriella O'Donnell (11) 22
Max Jenner (10) 23
Katie Clarke (11) 24
Amber Harney-Lichfield (11) 25
Joe Tyler (10) 26
Connor Summerfield (11) 27
Jade Probert (11) 28
Amber Charalambous (11) 29

Highfield School
Maddie Merryweather (10) 30
Chloe Lant (10) 31
Lily Streames-Smith (10) 32
Abigail Connor (10) 33

Rebecca Islam (10) 34
Georgina Wickham-Smith (10) 35
Paven Uppal (10) 36
Laura Dunn-Sims (9) 37
Elnaz Bedroud (10) 38
Alice Wood (10) 39
Olivia Thomson (10) 40
Grace Poynter (10) 41
Eleanor Slade (10) 42

Kingsnorth CE Primary School
Jack Sims (10) 43
Daniel Holland (10) 44
Natasha Francis (10) 45
Martin Nichols (10) 46
Kayleigh Winn (10) 47
Dominic Osbourne (10) 48
William Ashdown (10) 49
Katie Wright (10) 50
Callum Booth (10) 51

Langafel CE Primary School
Callum Halls (8) 52
Jared Bewsey (8) 53
Georgia Knight (7) 54
Callum Gibson (8) 55
Georgie Armstrong (8) 56

Grace Harris (8)	57
William Fifield (7)	58
Robbie Beard (7)	59
Jay Chambers (8)	60

Langton Green Primary School

Hannah Holway (11)	61
James Wakelin (11)	62
Rachel Edgar (11)	63
Bethany Lefevre (11)	64
Bethany Noble (11)	65
Connor McCabe (11)	66
Ryan Magee (11)	67
Lara Molnar (10)	68
Abigail Harman (11)	69
Nikki Bennett-Batey (11)	70
Charlotte Edwards (10)	71
Ella Davey (11)	72
Rhianna Steer (11)	73
Luke Stoneman (11)	74
Charlie Sapwell (11)	75
Rachel Jennings (11)	76
Ryan Searle (10)	77
Harrison Butcher (11)	78

Leigh Primary School

Lucy Doherty (7)	79
Leia Tiltman (6)	80

Marlborough House School

Charlie Gellett (10)	81
Oliver Bentsen (10)	82
Clementine Plummer (10)	83
Oscar Plomer-Roberts (9)	84
Gus Edmondson (10)	85
Elliot Gowers (10)	86
Henry Davies (9)	87
Ella Carr (10)	88
Jamie Tomalin (10)	89
James Weighell (10)	90
Charlie Hunter Blair (10)	91
Charles Macpherson (10)	92
Charles Snelling-Colyer (10)	93
Eloise Alikhani (10)	94
Henry Petch (10)	95

Milstead & Frinsted CE School

Rhiannon Wallwork (9)	96
Alfie Rouy (8)	97
Freya Rix (8)	98
Ricki Gibson (8)	99
David Jones (8)	100
Amber Town (8)	101
Thomas Bullock (7)	102
Nathan Brown (9)	103
Ryan Cay (9)	104
Joshua Mortiboys (9)	105
Scott Kerridge (9)	106
Jake Rix (7)	107
Jennifer Hook (10)	108
George Wright (9)	109
Harry Bassant (9)	110
James Cross (10)	111

Brandon Sladden (10) 112
Niamh Whittaker (10) 113
Rhys Archer (10) 114
Amia Town (10) 115

Minster CE Primary School
Julia Ferrett (10) 116

Northdown Primary School
Charley Hall (7) 117
Sarah Channing (11) 118
Daniel Bennett (11) 119
Liam McFetridge (11) 120
Zaakiyah Lagerdien (11) 121
Chelsea Sullivan (11) 122
Hannah Messenger (11) 123
Marcela Hickova (10) 124
Rebecca Edwards (11) 125
Lynn Butterfield (10) 126
Dominic Wallen (9) 127

Plaxtol Primary School
Joseph Chantree (10) 128
Jamie Rouse (10) 129
Charlie Pike (11) 130
Charlie Robertson (10) 131
Frances Peek (10) 132
Kieran Brown (11) 133
Jodie Jordan (10) 134
Jorden Fairweather (10) 135
Joshua Read (10) 136
James Freeman (10) 137

Jonathan Midgley (10) 138
Jessica Pallet (10) 139
Karl Egeland (9) 140

St Mary's Catholic Primary School, Gillingham
Grace Elliott (10) 141
Elena Margerison (10) 142
Katie Lepore (10) 143
Samuel Atkins (10) 144
Gemma Maxey (10) 145
Jade O'Connell (10) 146
Macauly McKenzie (10) 147
Rochelle Garcia (10) 148
Phoebe Vadgama (10) 149
Molly Weller (9) 150
Katie Rayner (10) 151
Claire Scholes (10) 152
Monica Chapinduka (10) 153
Shannon Rudden (10) 154
William Brittain (10) 155
Shamyla Jahangiri (10) 156

St Paul's CE Primary School, Swanley Village
Rachel Sutton (10) 157
Jack Gilbert (11) 158
Catherine Ashley-Smith (10) 159
Nicola Freeman (10) 160
Ryan Russell (11) 161
James Green (11) 162

Emmie Cason (11) 163
Sam Cason (10) 164
Thea Medland (10) 165
Nicholas Couvret (10) 166
Melina Tomas (10) 167
Carl Aylett (11).....................................168
Alice Spinola (11) 169
Thomas Franklin (10) 170
Harry Gilbert (10).................................171
Charlotte Summers (9)........................172
David Mason (10) 173

St Peter Chanel RC Primary School, Sidcup
Libby Vinten (9) 174
Toby Sanford (9)..................................175
Holly Dixon (9) 176
Jade Verrico (9) 177
Rebecca Harvey (9) 178
Jade Hutchinson (9) 179
Reece Wright (10) 180
Thomas Monaghan (10).......................181
Ela Kutereba (7) 182
Caitlin Wyatt (8)....................................183
Olivia Douglas (7) 184
Sophie Young (8) 185
Isabella Coleman (8) 186
Louise Rumble (8) 187
Francesca Hart (7) 188
Santini Holmes (6) 189
Erin Ferris (7) 190

Victoria O'Neill (7)................................191

St Simon of England RC (VA) Primary School, Ashford
Jerome Swan (8) 192
Ewen Rai (8) 193
Harry Dryland (7) 194
Ben Fraser (8).......................................195
Max May (8) 196
Luke Brooke (8) 197
Megan Fisher (8) 198
Emma Knight (8) 199
Claudia Knight (8) 200
Hannah Peirson (8) 201
Inithaa Mariyanayagam (7)..................202
Shakira Griffin (8).................................203
Jack Macdonald (8) 204
Georgia Belfiore (8) 205
Isabelle Lugg (8) 206
Monica Jarvis (8) 207
Tazmyn Burgess (8).............................208
Aimee Robinson (8).............................209
Sally Hazelwood (8) 210
Scott Dorman (8)..................................211
Ben Pali (7) 212
Danielle Rice (8) 213

St Stephen's Junior School, Canterbury
Nicholas Pearce (10) 214
Gwendy Grynfeld (11) 215
Grace Davis (11) 216
Jasmin Brown (10) 217

The Mini Sagas

Henry VII

There he stood before me, an English baron. Realising I had no money I looked around the room, I saw a beautiful portrait. I asked the baron, 'Sir, can I borrow that?'
'Yes my lord,' he replied and frowned. I walked out, laughing all the way to the palace.

Sophie Phillips (9)

Flying

I rose up, flying higher and higher. I soared with the birds gliding across the sky. A powerful light illuminated my back, warming me to the core. All too soon I landed on the sandy floor of the outdoor school of Callum Park Riding School, the jump long behind me.

Hannah Aldous (11)
Bligh Junior School

Birthday Surprise

Zac tiptoed down the stairs. Suddenly, he was reminded of his mother's words, 'Don't go into the cupboard'. He had to! He entered the kitchen. *Creak!* Zac gasped and turned to the stairs. Phew, he was safe. Zac opened the cupboard. *Splat!* Zac got what he deserved.

Rebecca Peard (11)
Bligh Junior School

The Scary Steps

I slowly stepped towards the old wooden door. It was about to close when I stopped it with my hand. It felt cold and damp. My hands were shaking. The haunted house was large. *Bang!* The haunted house was scary. I knew this was the wrong choice to choose.

Kelly Greenfield
Bligh Junior School

Jungle Boy

I walked through the jungle, over roots and under branches. I saw a woman getting attacked by a fierce lion. I ran as fast as my legs could take me. I took it down by the legs, the lady ran. I felt like a hero.
Tom, wake up,' yelled Mum.

Ben Carter (10)
Churchill CE Primary School

Ride Of Terror

'Come on Emma.' Emily grabbed my arm.
'But I'm scared,' I argued.
'I'll be right with you, please?' Emily said trying to persuade me.
'All right,' I agreed nervously stepping onto the ride.
'Here we go.'
We twirled then we stopped.
'Thanks for riding the tea cups,' a speaker announced.

Emma Fitch (11)
Churchill CE Primary School

Tiny Tales Fiction From Kent

My Fear

I sat in the seat, my hands clenched to the safety bar. It started and spun around and then up and down. It started to slow down, the man got me out of the seat. I was relieved that I had overcome my fear of the dreaded tea cup ride.

Harry Bond (11)
Churchill CE Primary School

Humpty Dumpty!

Eating ice cream Humpty Dumpty sat on the wall. Suddenly, Bumpty came and pushed Humpty off! Bumpty quickly ran away. All the king's horses and all the king's men tried to put Humpty together but it was too late. Humpty was in too many pieces.

Bethany Taylor (11)
Churchill CE Primary School

Tiny Tales Fiction From Kent

Sam's Fear

Sam was a 10-year-old boy. He had a fear, the fear was the evil witch's house. People talked about it all the time. He decided to cross the forest and search the house.
Soon he was there, he went in and the witch wasn't there, it wasn't true.

Baldeep Chahal (10)
Churchill CE Primary School

Help, I'm Scared!

Lucy came in from school, the house was empty except for her older sister upstairs. There was music from her sister's room. She went to see her. She wasn't there, she heard voices. 'Hello?' she screamed. Footsteps came to her bedroom, her sister came in.
'What? I've been shopping.'

Gabriella O'Donnell (11)
Churchill CE Primary School

Crash!

Bang! 'What was that?' said Joanne.
'I don't know, just go back to sleep,' begged Harry.
The next morning when they woke up everything had been demolished.
'We've been robbed,' shouted Joanne.
'Try and stay calm please,' said Harry.
Knock-knock, 'Who's that?'
'The police,' shouted Harry and Joanne.

Max Jenner (10)
Churchill CE Primary School

It Was A …

I finished riding my pony in the sand school. I untacked her and put her in the stable and walked back to my house. I went on the computer and I found my horse with a message saying, 'You horse will die'.
Argh! I awoke, it was a nightmare!

Katie Clarke (11)
Churchill CE Primary School

Tiny Tales Fiction From Kent

The Disturbance

Thunder boomed and lightning bolted. Sarah was beginning to feel very scared. A sudden shiver ran up her spine. Sarah started to walk a bit faster and faster until she was sprinting. Sarah tripped and fell, something had grabbed her leg, she couldn't get free …

Amber Harney-Lichfield (11)
Churchill CE Primary School

T-Rex And Triceratops

Once, seventy million years ago, there was a T-Rex who was hungry. He was hiding quietly in the bushes, he was about to jump on a massive triceratops only two metres away from him. So he leapt into the air and slashed at the triceratops. Blood dripped down.

Joe Tyler (10)
Churchill CE Primary School

The Chase

It began, I started running, it was gaining on me, closer, closer. I dared not look behind me.
'Come here little boy,' he chanted.
'N-no-no.' I ran down an alleyway. 'I think I've lost him,' I said in my brain.
I turned around and there he was. 'Argh!'

Connor Summerfield (11)
Churchill CE Primary School

Bored

I dropped the powder in the pot, it fell and then I sat waiting, bored as a tree in a city. So lonely in my own world of fun. Then I heard 'Jade, Jade?'
It was my teacher, the lesson was over!

Jade Probert (11)
Churchill CE Primary School

Tiny Tales Fiction From Kent

Crocodile

'Argh, help, help, argh!' I was falling, turning upside-down. Swerving, tilting, swooshing, swirling. I was on a crocodile, trying to survive the terrifying ride of the crocodile's tail. As I called for help, the handlebars went back. The crocodile roller coaster ride had stopped.

Amber Charalambous (11)
Churchill CE Primary School

Spots

A puppy was very beautiful, she had a white silky coat. 'Oh no,' she said. 'A spot, and another, they're multiplying. I'll go to the vet's!' She had a check-up. Her mother went to see if she was there. 'I've got spots,' the puppy wailed.

'But you're a Dalmatian!'

Maddie Merryweather (10)
Highfield School

Tiny Tales Fiction From Kent

Come As An Angel

Emma wanted to come as twins to the party.
She sent me a text: come as an angle. I hurried
to the party wearing a massive triangle.
'Why are you wearing that?'
'You said come as an angle!'
'I meant come as an angel! You know I can't
spell well!'

Chloe Lant (10)
Highfield School

Oh No

There once was a chief who had warts everywhere. He went to a witch's house and stole a potion. He drank the whole bottle. His warts went. Off to the ball he drove, but five seconds later he developed chickenpox while he was dancing with the queen of his island!

Lily Streames-Smith (10)
Highfield School

Untitled

The old wizard tried to make a spell to get rid of his spot on his nose. Some spells made his nose hairy, pink and pointy. He mixed the blue sky with the yellow sun potion. He poured it on his nose. Then his nose grew and grew for evermore.

Abigail Connor (10)
Highfield School

The Professor's New Potion

Bang! Crash! Sorry about that, it's the professor and his new equipment. I'm Berty, the dragon, the professor's pet.
'I've done it, I've made the potion to make myself younger.' The professor drank it.
Uh oh. 'Professor, you're so young, now you're a baby. Professor, you have gone, you've disappeared.'

Rebecca Islam (10)
Highfield School

Tiny Tales Fiction From Kent

Biology

Julie got home from school and went into her garden. She found something very strange. It was a tall, spiky flower. It snapped at her. 'Ouch!' cried Julie. She rushed to the shed and got the scissors and sliced it off.
'Julie, that was my science project,' wailed her sister.

Georgina Wickham-Smith (10)
Highfield School

The Messenger

Matthew had a parrot. The parrot passed messages. Matthew told the parrot to say to Connor to stand up to the school bully, but the parrot said Matthew said Connor was a bully. Matthew and Connor were friends, but now, worst enemies. Thanks to the parrot, the worst ever messenger.

Paven Uppal (10)
Highfield School

Tiny Tales Fiction From Kent

Unfair

It was sports day at Henry's school. Henry knew he would win his events. Everyone else did too. He won five gold medals.
'It's so unfair,' said Marie.
'No it's not,' said Henry.
Henry asked Gran why everyone said it's so unfair?
'Henry, you are the headmaster,' said Gran.

Laura Dunn-Sims (9)
Highfield School

Bogey Boy

I was standing in the audition room, actually singing. I sat outside and waited for the judges to choose wh'd play lead in the film. They called me back into the room. I was shocked when they said, 'You've got the part as the boy eating all his friends' bogeys!'

Elnaz Bedroud (10)
Highfield School

The Bug Hunt

Lucy was walking through the park. She found a weird beetle. She brought it to her school. Her science teacher said it was a three-legged ladybird and there were only two in the world because they live for 100 years. Then she dropped it in the pool. It drowned.

Alice Wood (10)
Highfield School

Green Dad

Polly got back to the tree and found that her dad was green. 'Why are you green? You're normally brown,' she said.
'Don't worry,' her dad said. 'Don't you think this colour suits me?'
'How do you do that Dad?' said Polly.
'You do realise that we are chameleons, Polly?'

Olivia Thomson (10)
Highfield School

Disappointed

I woke up on Saturday morning. It was a special day because I had an audition in London. I arrived there and I walked in. I performed in front of four judges. They looked impressed. I sang and did some scenes.
Wow … I had the part of a donkey's bottom!

Grace Poynter (10)
Highfield School

Love At First Sight

'Would you like to dance Cinderella?' said the prince.
'Oh yes please,' said Cinderella.
'Wow, who is that beautiful girl?' asked the prince.
'That's my ugly sister,' said Cinderella.
Ugly? She is the most beautiful girl I've ever seen,' he said. 'Can you introduce me to her?' he said nervously.

Eleanor Slade (10)
Highfield School

Tiny Tales Fiction From Kent

Aliens Vs Earth

1974, aliens attacked Earth. UFOs were found in Washington. Eight aliens came out. They were heading for the White House. First police tried to stop them but failed. The president shot … *bang!* The president killed two aliens. *Bang!* President dead. Aliens renamed Earth and called it Bogies.

'Jack, wake up!'

Jack Sims (10)
Kingsnorth CE Primary School

The Scared Dinosaur

One day a T-rex was on a journey to the sea. Then he spotted a shadow following him and it looked familiar. It looked just like him. Whatever he did, the shadow did. He was scared like never before. He ran home. Then he realised it was his shadow.

Daniel Holland (10)
Kingsnorth CE Primary School

Tiny Tales Fiction From Kent

Wow!

One day a boy called James and his grandad Roger went fishing in Loch Ness. They lived in Scotland too. Roger started to snooze, James saw something. *He caught a huge fish!* And the Loch Ness monster with it!

'Wow, look Grandad.'

He looked again, it was his imagination.

Natasha Francis (10)
Kingsnorth CE Primary School

The TV Monster

I hate the monster in this TV! I hope he will not find me … *bang, bang, bang!* The monster came. I ran and ran around the screen but there wasn't much space. I was getting tired. Then I realised it was my brother chasing me in his monster suit!

Martin Nichols (10)
Kingsnorth CE Primary School

Prehistoric!

Charlie crept through the jungle, he wasn't a man anymore, he was a prehistoric triceratops. He bumped into a tree, but it wasn't a tree … it was a T-Rex. He ran for it, then … 'Mum, Charlie made my party dress muddy!'
'Charlie!'
The mother T-Rex is coming, *run!*

Kayleigh Winn (10)
Kingsnorth CE Primary School

The Lost Ruby Of The King

Fred was guarding the king's ruby room. He heard a scream, Fred unlocked the door. It was gone! Fred knew who had stolen the ruby. The thief had left a glove. Fred knew who it belonged to, Bob the cook! He arrested Bob - the ruby was returned to the king.

Dominic Osbourne (10)
Kingsnorth CE Primary School

The Spooky Mansion

One evening I heard a scream coming out of a mansion. I checked it out, I saw a glowing green alien. I walked behind the alien. A ghost appeared. An alien said, 'Get out of the picture!' I shouted, 'I didn't know it was a picture!' Although it was.

William Ashdown (10)
Kingsnorth CE Primary School

Fame!

The fans were screaming! I was at the premier of 'Danger'. My stilettos were amazingly loud. I could barely walk. Being famous is hard! Suddenly … a gust of wind blew me over. 'You should be doing your homework, not playing in my stilettos!' Mum just spoilt my moment of *fame!*

Katie Wright (10)
Kingsnorth CE Primary School

Tiny Tales Fiction From Kent

The Covent Bomb

'Troops, go to Section B,' said Commander Callum. 'Our last time to do this. Must destroy the Covent bomb and the Covent!'
'We could get blown up!'
'Hurry up, go now!'
'Wake up Callum, this is maths not daydream time. You have a detention!' said Mr Taylor.
Hmmmm!

Callum Booth (10)
Kingsnorth CE Primary School

The Four Little Pigs

There were four little pigs. Their mum said to them, 'Go away and build a house of your own.' So they did what she said. One made a wooden house, another made a stick house, another made a stone house. The last made a brick house.

Callum Halls (8)
Langafel CE Primary School

Attack In The Woods

Someone called Jack went for an adventure. Jack met his friend Mick in the woods. They both met a zombie so they threw food at him. The zombie was not happy so he wrapped them up in paper. The soldiers shot the zombie down. The children ran home, fast!

Jared Bewsey (8)
Langafel CE Primary School

The Red Pony

There was a red pony. She got stuck in a hole, she was screaming for help. Some time later a little girl came past and heard the red pony. The little girl went to see her. She used a rope to help the pony, she got her out of there.

Georgia Knight (7)
Langafel CE Primary School

The New Neighbour

There were new next-door neighbours. The husband came over and had a moan because of the noise of the dog. His phone started to ring and he dropped it on the floor. The dog started to bark, it smashed into millions of pieces. So he stormed back home.

Callum Gibson (8)
Langafel CE Primary School

Ghost Thief

Once there was a girl called Sam and she went camping. That night she saw a boy drowning at this campsite. She was scared. Then she went to bed and saw her watch disappear. The next day she explored and saw a boy floating on water.

Georgie Armstrong (8)
Langafel CE Primary School

Tom And Alice With Their Friends

There once lived Alice and her three friends, Grace, Sidney and Emily. They all had annoying brothers. Tom, Stanley, Haydn and George. They all went to Bluewater for Tom and Alice's joint birthday. They went to Claire's and Game, had something to eat in TGI Fridays then went home.

Grace Harris (8)
Langafel CE Primary School

Untitled

One day there was a big jungle. In the centre of the jungle there was a big river. All of the animals went there for a drink.
One day there was a new crocodile. The crocodile owned the river. Every time you went you got hurt. No one went back.

William Fifield (7)
Langafel CE Primary School

Tiny Tales Fiction From Kent

Going To The Moon

One day a boy called Will was going to the moon with a man called Ron.
Five days later he took off, he got to the moon.
He saw an alien. 'Run!' said Ron.
'Argh! Scream, yes but run Will! and yes, scream as loud as you can.'

Robbie Beard (7)
Langafel CE Primary School

Hartley De Sales

One day we had a football match. We won 6-0. After the match our manager said we were the best players. We all had a big party. After that, we did some training. We had a very, very good time. It was the best!

Jay Chambers (8)
Langafel CE Primary School

Bermuda Dreams

I splashed and struggled gasping for air. The saltiness of the sparkly sea stung my eyes. 'Help!' I cried. 'Help!' Suddenly I saw a massive boat coming towards me. It read: *Bermuda Dreams Cruiser.* I swam, with all my might and grabbed the side of the boat. I was saved.

Hannah Holway (11)
Langton Green Primary School

The Terrible Tomb

Lee suddenly woke up to find himself in an ancient tomb. He looked around, he was in a candlelit tomb. Shadows of tall dark creatures behind the corners of the spooky corridors. He screamed murderously. Out of the corner of his eye he saw the walls slowly coming together …

James Wakelin (11)
Langton Green Primary School

Tiny Tales Fiction From Kent

Haunted

A shiver ran down my spine as I crept through the house. Cobwebs dangled from every corner of the house. I dodged them. Suddenly, my stomach lurched as I went down.
Finally, with my feet firmly back on the ground, I looked up to find I was trapped!

Rachel Edgar (11)
Langton Green Primary School

Shadow Mystery

Petrified, Alexis ran from the dark shadow that was haunting her that night. She crept slowly towards her mum's room. She wasn't there! The shadow looked just like her mum. The next morning she woke up. Nobody was there. Was it her mum or a ghost? She would never know!

Bethany Lefevre (11)
Langton Green Primary School

Tiny Tales Fiction From Kent

I

After queuing for the blasting ride, we finally got to the seats and sat down. We got ready, we went up the hill then left the station and leaned over the edge. It stopped. We all panicked. It was a power-cut. After five hours we fell!

Bethany Noble (11)
Langton Green Primary School

Silent Assassin

Silent assassin ran down the Empire State Building then down below in the murky alleyway. I saw a tramp with a bag of money. I jumped down and cut his neck with fibre wire. I also strangled him. His bleeding head rolled down the high street. He was dead!

Connor McCabe (11)
Langton Green Primary School

Darkness

I sat up … I was in my bed in the middle of the night. I needed a drink. My bones were heaved out of bed as I slid out. My feet hit the cold, hard floor. Suddenly, I was tripped over. Something grabbed my body. I was trapped!

Ryan Magee (11)
Langton Green Primary School

The Stag

I ran in and there stood the magnificent stag, standing there, glowing. Then it butted me into the wall and said in a deep low voice, 'You are dying, dying.'
Then my vision faded until finally it was gone. My head hit the dusty floor as I fainted …

Lara Molnar (10)
Langton Green Primary School

The Soul's Curse

I crept gingerly, dodging gravestones which lay ahead. I started to shake vigorously, it was a full moon. However, I still couldn't see and … I fell lower and lower until I was deep underground. I had awoken the souls, something was touching me. What was it? I never found out.

Abigail Harman (11)
Langton Green Primary School

The Beast Mother

She steadily walked up to the cave door. Amanda opened it, went on her knees straight away, started to crawl. Under obstacles, over objects. Amanda found a giant, a big beast. Luckily the beast was sleeping. Amanda crawled under the beast's bed. The beast woke.

'What are you doing darling, Amanda?'

Nikki Bennett-Batey (11)
Langton Green Primary School

The Devil Angel

It was a warm sunny day on the beach when two girls stepped into the sea. The weather then grew rainy and stormy. The girls ran out of the sea but were found to be lifted by an angel and suddenly dropped in a big swirl in the ocean …

Charlotte Edwards (10)
Langton Green Primary School

Emptiness

Creak! I opened the rusty metal door. The cold air eked slowly into the isolated room - I stepped inside. The freezing air brushed against my petite face. I gasped, amazed by the shining white island in front of my ice-blue eyes. I was in Antarctica.

Ella Davey (11)
Langton Green Primary School

Tiny Tales Fiction From Kent

Why? Why? Why?

As I trembled swimming through the Pacific Ocean I plunged through a beautiful cottage. I peered around, it was the only cottage. *But why was it in the middle of the Pacific Ocean?* I thought to myself. *It might be an old building. Why was it the only one here?*

Rhianna Steer (11)
Langton Green Primary School

The Stomach-Turning Murder, Vomit Projecting

The man slowly walked over to me, needle in his hand as sharp as a razor blade. I couldn't move, my hands tied behind my back. He slipped his hand onto my neck and slowly pulled my head up. He stabbed the needle into my eyelid and began to sew.

Luke Stoneman (11)
Langton Green Primary School

Tiny Tales Fiction From Kent

The Little Pirate

'Ah me bucko. I be Captain Todd of the Red Go-Kart and you'll be helping me find treasure. Let us go onwards past the great rock of the sofa and enter the bowl of treasure. Why do they taste like dog biscuits?'

Charlie Sapwell (11)
Langton Green Primary School

The Gravestones

Gingerly I crept through gravestones, dodging them cautiously so I didn't wake souls from their sleep. I glanced at the names and saw my own engraved in bold print. Hattie Queensworth 18.7.07. But hang on, wasn't that today? I felt a cold knife in my back. I keeled over, dead!

Rachel Jennings (11)
Langton Green Primary School

Storm God

He succeeded, he found the ruby. He was walking home when all the plants rotted. He thought, *what was going on?* He heard an evil laugh, he peered up. He saw a devil drifting out the sky. Everything went dark. A flash of lightning struck, this time it struck him …

Ryan Searle (10)
Langton Green Primary School

The Berserker

Thump, thump, thump! The inhuman creature was stomping very close to my hiding place. I could almost smell its ragged breath. I could hear myself shaking in fear. Then all of a sudden it saw me and ran with such speed. I couldn't run, then it all went black!

Harrison Butcher (11)
Langton Green Primary School

The Mysterious Castle

In a beautiful land, a little cottage stood. Inside lived hardworking children. One night they were invited into the nearby castle. They were met by a preposterous knight who protected a small girl called Mandy. They wanted to take her home with them. The knight would not allow it

...

Lucy Doherty (7)
Leigh Primary School

The Magic Stone

There were some cousins, they were walking in a forest and picked up a stone and threw it. It turned into a diamond. When they got home no one was there. They heard a noise, it was footsteps going upstairs. Someone was after the diamond.

Leia Tiltman (6)
Leigh Primary School

A Soccer Shocker

The ref blew his whistle, the match began. The first half was full of chances but Liverpool failed to score and Palace could not either. The second half was much better. Liverpool's defence was worn down. Marco Reich scored for Crystal Palace! Ref blew his whistle. *The crowd went wild!*

Charlie Gellett (10)
Marlborough House School

Robin Hood

One hot summer's day, Robin Hood went in his new Formula 1 car with his x3 rifle to steal from the poor and give to the rich.
The next day the poor chased after him and Robin said, 'I'm not doing that again,' and went back home for tea.

Oliver Bentsen (10)
Marlborough House School

Tiny Tales Fiction From Kent

Humpty Dumpty

Humpty Dumpty was allergic to dogs, he saw one and sneezed, *atishoo!* He suddenly fell off the wall, the shell cracked. Yolk fell out and he sadly died. Gallons of yolk poured out and the dog who was watching drank the yolk and was sick. More clearing up, *noooo!*

Clementine Plummer (10)
Marlborough House School

The Tortoise And The Hare

Tortoise set off, Hare followed closely behind him. Tortoise thought, *you can never ever catch me!* Suddenly Hare overtook him. 'Why did you do that?' Suddenly the nitrous tanks went off. Hare was gently running along and then he saw a fast flying tortoise. The tortoise won, the hare fainted!

Oscar Plomer-Roberts (9)
Marlborough House School

Wilma Short Stories

Wilma was stuck in an ice tower in the North Pole. A prince decided to save her. He visited every day and said, 'Wilma, Wilma, what shall I do? How do I save you? Wilma I've got it, I'll lift up the tower and put it in a rainforest. Yes!'

Gus Edmondson (10)
Marlborough House School

At Marlborough

Day one at Marlborough. A disaster, my chair broke, I fell and hurt my bum.
Day two. Of course, ink in my eye, it was true agony, now I am partly colour blind.
Day three. Flew down some stairs, cracked my nose and broke a cheek bone, it really hurt.

Elliot Gowers (10)
Marlborough House School

Tiny Tales Fiction From Kent

Little Red Riding Hood

Little Red Riding Hood was delivering cakes to her granny. She met a wolf and he asked for some cakes. She shooed him away. She got to her granny's house and found a wolf in disguise. Her granny was attacking him.
'Aren't you eating Granny?'
'No, I am a vegetarian!'

Henry Davies (9)
Marlborough House School

The Ugly Duckling

The egg cracks … *yuck!* What is that little thing? Get out of my sight. The ugly duckling waddles away sadly.

One day a beautiful swan comes by. 'I'm your so-called ugly duckling, aren't I beautiful? I'm a magnificent swan now! I'm going to play with my friends now, bye!'

Ella Carr (10)
Marlborough House School

Tiny Tales Fiction From Kent

The Sprint

It is time for sports day and time for the sprint race. The competitors line up at the start. 'On your marks, ready, steady go.'
They are off. But what's this? A masked boy, steaming past everyone, but oh no, he's sprinting into a rabbit hole!
'Oh, that looks painful.'

Jamie Tomalin (10)
Marlborough House School

The Two Red Squirrels And The Grey Squirrel

The two red squirrels built two houses. The first out of weeds, the second out of paper. The evil grey squirrel came, put weed killer on the house. The first squirrel ran to the second squirrel's house. The grey squirrel wet the paper house. Both the red squirrels got eaten.

James Weighell (10)
Marlborough House School

The Pie-Eating Competition

One day at Benenden Primary School there was a pie-eating competition. Big Billy Bomber versus Tiny Timmy Tinnee. They were off! Both of them scoffing the pies one after the other! Could there be an upset? Could Tiny Timmy Tinnee win? Wait - he passed out, Bomber won!

Charlie Hunter Blair (10)
Marlborough House School

The History Tree

There's an old tree in my garden. Looking up through the branches, I noticed Queen Victoria. Next some World War II soldiers ran past. A Saxon odour wafted through the air. All at once these images turned back into simple shapes in the foliage. I was left with my thoughts.

Charles Macpherson (10)
Marlborough House School

The Haircut

Once in a land far, far away, a beautiful princess Rapunzel was trapped in a tower. A witch had cursed her. The prince had tried to climb up to save her. 'Rapunzel, Rapunzel, let down your golden hair!'
'I can't, I went to the hairdresser's yesterday!'
'Therein lies a problem!'

Charles Snelling-Colyer (10)
Marlborough House School

Jack And The Beanstalk

A boy had been in trade for his cow; boy got a spanking from his mother because of this trade. Crying, boy kissed the bean, threw it out his window. Next day boy saw his bean. It was colossal! Boy climbed up the plant and met a beautiful girl.

Eloise Alikhani (10)
Marlborough House School

Tiny Tales Fiction From Kent

The Danger Button

The race is finally starting. *Go!* Tortoise zooming down the track at 1mph. Cheetah tearing the ground at 1,763mph. Tortoise knocked out from exhaustion. Suddenly squirrel presses danger button. Everything turns upside down. Cheetah is knocked out and Tortoise is going 1,763mph, the ground on fire. Tortoise wins!

Henry Petch (10)
Marlborough House School

Alone Again

I never had a friend before, until this winter. He was like a Christmas present. I made him but he was still my best friend. I gave him, hat, scarf and gloves. I told him to stay but it was no use. He still went.
Nature took my snowman friend.

Rhiannon Wallwork (9)
Milstead & Frinsted CE School

Mummy

Walking nervously through the low-ceiling tunnels, suddenly a massive rock came tumbling past me. I screamed extremely loudly, a mummy appeared out of a back tomb. From behind me it picked me up and put me in a black gloomy tomb, by his fingertips, into the pitch-black tomb!

Alfie Rouy (8)
Milstead & Frinsted CE School

Last Leap

She was fast, but not fast enough. The gazelle jumped and ducked. She was tired, but could not give up. The lion was cunning, taking shortcuts and jumping ahead of her. She lost her footing, she fell, singing her very last cry. The lion pounced. She heard her last heartbeat.

Freya Rix (8)
Milstead & Frinsted CE School

Tiny Tales Fiction From Kent

Untitled

One dark misty night, a howling sound reached my ears. An image of a werewolf formed in the fog, frightening me half to death. A flame of fire was shivering, getting closer and closer until … there emerged … the silhouette of a fire cat.

Ricki Gibson (8)
Milstead & Frinsted CE School

Who's There?

Bang! went the door. She slowly opened it, no one there but the dark - eerie. She shut out the creepy night. *Bang!* went the door, hesitantly the woman opened it. No one there, then a voice - a voice spoke. 'Ha, ha, trick or treat?'

David Jones (8)
Milstead & Frinsted CE School

The First Time

Way up high, going round in circles. Then, I got faster, up and down, up and down. Squeezing its tummy a bit. We went zooming past the fences. 'Woah there,' I demanded. We stood nervously looked at the pole. *Jump!* We landed. 'Good boy Lordy!' Now I can ride horses.

Amber Town (8)
Milstead & Frinsted CE School

Untitled

Smack! went our new door. Who was that? I opened the door. 'Who's there? Hello,' I said, 'anyone there?'

No, nothing, probably just the wind. I closed the door. *Bang!* The door flew open. 'What's happening?' Someone said, 'Trick or treat?' 'Ha, ha, ha, that was funny, ha!'

Thomas Bullock (7)
Milstead & Frinsted CE School

Untitled

One dark gloomy night I was walking in a field. Just then the bushy grass started to rattle. My heart started to beat like a drum. Closer, closer and closer … I moved apprehensively towards the noise but … it was just a bunny rabbit. Now I know my fear of rabbits.

Nathan Brown (9)
Milstead & Frinsted CE School

Untitled

It was cold but the heater was on. Suddenly, the heater turned on and off … Archie was shivering head to toe. Archie was terrified, he thought it was a nightmare. He started to pinch himself. Quickly the door slammed and an unusual shadow appeared. 'Surprise, Dad, it's 8am in the morning!'
'Oh!'

Ryan Cay (9)
Milstead & Frinsted CE School

Tiny Tales Fiction From Kent

Untitled

It was hot, but the fan was on. Suddenly the fan turned on, off, on, off. Archie was horrified. He was tingling from head to toe. Thinking it was a nightmare he started to pinch himself. The door started to slam - an unusual shadow appeared.
'Surprise Mum, it's 7am.'

Joshua Mortiboys (9)
Milstead & Frinsted CE School

The Dark Night

Bang! The door slammed. 'There's someone here right in my room,' whispered Ron. All he could see was a room of darkness. Shadows the shape of people, Ron was frightened head to toe. *Crack!* A bolt of lightning struck. 'Happy Birthday Ron!' but who was that in the dark?

Scott Kerridge (9)
Milstead & Frinsted CE School

Tiny Tales Fiction From Kent

The Creature

Jimmy held his breath. He knew any minute now he would be found. He heard a screech. It was coming closer. Suddenly a giant eye peered through the gap. He screamed. He knew any minute he would be snatched up for dinner. The creature suddenly disappeared. Jimmy was safe.

Jake Rix (7)
Milstead & Frinsted CE School

The Loch Ness Monster

Suddenly a slimy worm-like creature rolled out of the murky water with its tail flicking behind it. In a matter of seconds the mysterious creature dived under and crept along the bottom of the lake. It darted out of the water in a rolling motion with a thunderous bump.

Jennifer Hook (10)
Milstead & Frinsted CE School

Tiny Tales Fiction From Kent

Untitled

The ship was being tossed and turned in the monster waves. It was rocking all night until I saw a tail flick up from the monster water. I was scared for a moment and until I knew it was Nessy. It had a long pointy tail. Then it went back.

George Wright (9)
Milstead & Frinsted CE School

Boomballabeam

It was my sister's birthday. It was very boring for me because there were mostly girls there. Suddenly there was a knock at the door. I ran to get it but my sister beat me.

Later, when the magician set up, he said the wrong magic spell, 'Heinz Salad Cream!'

Harry Bassant (9)
Milstead & Frinsted CE School

Tiny Tales Fiction From Kent

Dinosaurs

I looked around the corner and I did not believe what I saw. I spotted an object in the undergrowth. It was moving very fast, I thought it was a dog but no, it was much bigger. Then I saw it was a dinosaur, but not very big.

James Cross (10)
Milstead & Frinsted CE School

Untitled

Zoom - it landed on Earth, the door opened, out came a Dalek shouting, 'Exterminate the Doctor, exterminate … '

To their surprise there were hundreds of holograms. Doctor the real Doctor was in his TARDIS planning his escape to planet Jolly. No, we had got a power cut, everywhere was in darkness.

Brandon Sladden (10)
Milstead & Frinsted CE School

The Wild Hound

Suddenly a greyhound baring his teeth ripped the hare from the ground. The squeaking of the animal was vile. There were scars down his back, one scar over his eye. He pounced back into the undergrowth with a howl and a scream of the animal in his jaws.

Niamh Whittaker (10)
Milstead & Frinsted CE School

Black Rodeo

Tom was shaking with fear. He looked at his watch. He looked around the sandy desert.
'5, 4, 3, 2, 1,' Tom said and this strange sound rang in Tom's head.
A UFO appeared and an alien walked out with a laser. Tom said fearfully, 'I'm ready.'
Zap!
'Argh!'

Rhys Archer (10)
Milstead & Frinsted CE School

Tiny Tales Fiction From Kent

Pegasus Adventure

Natalie soared through the starry sky on the back of Pegasus. The pink clouds flew past. Time seemed to have paused. Suddenly, Pegasus jolted and Natalie slipped off the horse's silky back. She plunged through the air and hit a soft comfy ground. Natalie found herself in her beautiful bedroom.

Amia Town (10)
Milstead & Frinsted CE School

The Mad Class

On the first day of Year Six I walked into the classroom. My class was mad! I couldn't believe I was stuck with these loonies. Fred was throwing paper. There's that gang that think they're so hard but when they get threatened they act like a bunch of headless chickens.

Julia Ferrett (10)
Minster CE Primary School

The Smoky Room

The room started to fill with smoke, it was getting thicker and thicker. You could hardly see. The smoke alarm started wailing, ringing in my ears. All of a sudden a figure appeared through the smoke. It was Dave. 'Dinner's ready,' he said.

Charley Hall (7)
Northdown Primary School

The Spell Goes Wrong

There was a witch called Witchhansel. She got told to do a spell by her teacher, Miss Blueberry. She had to make a mouse turn into a mug! She mixed a potion, *puff!* Witchhansel said, 'Oh no.'
'What have you done?' asked Miss Blueberry.
'Nothing Miss,' she replied.
Bang! Puff!

Sarah Channing (11)
Northdown Primary School

Untitled

Hey Diddle Diddle cat had a wonderful magical fiddle. The spotted old cow jumped over the shiny golden moon. The large ancient bloodhound croakily laughed to see such a sight! The dirty spoon ran off with the glamorous embarrassed dish again, only to never return to their friends again.

Daniel Bennett (11)
Northdown Primary School

The Weird Football Game

Kick-off! Spoony passes to Spiggs. He shoots! Keeper saves it! Spoony shoots with one of his elastic legs. This game could be over because Mars bars are leading 1-0. The flying heads need to score fast. Spoony stretches, oh no, he's scored! What a disaster. The crowd cheers.

Liam McFetridge (11)
Northdown Primary School

Tiny Tales Fiction From Kent

Baa Baa Black Sheep

'Have you any wool?' said the man. 'Yes, but not for you!' said the sheep. 'Only for the master, the dame and the boy who lives down the lane.' Then the sheep was attacked by a thief. Sheep pulled out his water pistol and fired it! He's now safe.

Zaakiyah Lagerdien (11)
Northdown Primary School

The Aliens

Bang! Something had just caused the biggest bang ever. As people awoke the weird creatures travelled the city, terrorising everything. The officer screamed at them for making such a mess with their disgusting long bodies. Then the creatures decided to eat the officer-like cake. Luckily the aliens left!

Chelsea Sullivan (11)
Northdown Primary School

Tiny Tales Fiction From Kent

When The Dog Once Played A Fiddle

When the dog once played a fiddle, the tune was Hey Diddle Diddle. A cow jumped extremely high! Suddenly a cute kitten laughed really loud because she thought she saw such amusement. So the shiny silver dish ran away with the fork and said, 'Will he play that tune again?'

Hannah Messenger (11)
Northdown Primary School

Lynn And Marla - The River

Tony and I were playing in my mum's beautiful garden. We were building a river. I put some bricks on the high land. Tony had put some wet soil and made sort of a hole. Then together we poured some water over the bricks. It was like a real river.

Marcela Hickova (10)
Northdown Primary School

Something!

Midnight, the punters had gone. The pub owner slept silently, when he heard noises. Cautiously he moved like a mouse looking around. 'Hello?' Soundless! As he went to bed he saw something, it was motionless. The man phoned the police. When they arrived the only noise was the toilets flushing.

Rebecca Edwards (11)
Northdown Primary School

Disappearing Act

Just as the door to the spooky mansion closed, I heard someone whispering. It got clearer as I tiptoed nearer. I listened and it certainly wasn't what I expected. Then someone grabbed me, I tried to get away, but the next thing I knew I was gone!

Lynn Butterfield (10)
Northdown Primary School

The Penguins In The Desert, Literally

Some penguins lived in custard. One day it was tipped out and cooked. One penguin got stuck on a spoon, another penguin called emergency services. 'My friend is going to be eaten.' 'Thank you for calling emergency services, your call has been placed in a queue … '
'No!'

Dominic Wallen (9)
Northdown Primary School

Attack Of The Dragon

I went to sleep. I was St George in 1692. There was a dragon! It was emerald-green, its scales sparkling. It launched at me. Gliding through the air. Just in time I drew my sword to deflect from the claws. It got me!
I woke up. It was a dream.

Joseph Chantree (10)
Plaxtol Primary School

The Forest

Me and my friend went for a walk in an enchanted forest. We all followed a fox to see where it went. Suddenly it led us to a big patch of flowers and all sorts. There was a cabin, beside it was a house. We weren't alone on the island ...

Jamie Rouse (10)
Plaxtol Primary School

The Woodcutter

A house in the middle of a wood had been lived in for a year by the woodcutter with his wife and daughter called Marie. She ran away! She found a door in a bush and opened it. She was in a pleasant land. She lived in it for evermore.

Frances Peek (10)
Plaxtol Primary School

Tiny Tales Fiction From Kent

The Claw

The scary claw was getting closer and closer, it lunged at me but I dodged it in time. Something was strange about it, it was oozing green blood. It wrapped around my neck and it made me choke. It squeezed me. I hit the hand, I fell into the pit.

Kieran Brown (11)
Plaxtol Primary School

The Friendly Bear

There was a kind bear called Fred. When he was walking in the woods he got tired and found a cosy spot to sleep. After three hours he woke up and people were staring at him! He was scared when he saw them. But the people were afraid.

Jodie Jordan (10)
Plaxtol Primary School

Tiny Tales Fiction From Kent

Me And My Sister Went To The Forest

One day me and my sister went out to the forest. We got about halfway when all of a sudden it got dark, we heard noises and saw gloomy eyes, instantly we saw a movement, then some light. So we ran home and told our mum and dad.

Jorden Fairweather (10)
Plaxtol Primary School

The Woods

Me and my friends, Jamie, Jack and Jens, went into the wood, we found a pit, I went down, my friends followed me. We found a swamp. On the other side there was a treasure chest. We crossed the swamp, but when we crossed it there was no way back.

Joshua Read (10)
Plaxtol Primary School

Tiny Tales Fiction From Kent

A Tasty Possession

Tim was a young boy who bought a piece of corn. He found it granted wishes! He wished for a better wooden house and money for his family.

His mum threw the corn away as it was stale! Tim was cursed with bad luck for the rest of his life!

James Freeman (10)
Plaxtol Primary School

Sphynx Vs Pharaoh

Over a thousand years ago there lived a pharaoh, the creator of the sphynx. When it was finished it came alive. The pharaoh had to fight the sphynx using his tablet. The pharaoh ended the battle by freeing it.
The sphynx is still plotting after another thousand years.

Jonathan Midgley (10)
Plaxtol Primary School

The Bold Strong Knight

Once there was a maiden who had been locked up with a witch! Then one day a knight tried to find her! He did! But he was caught too! They made an escape and got away. They married. The king made the forest better and arrested the witch.

Jessica Pallet (10)
Plaxtol Primary School

The Huge Red-Eyed Owl In Africa

The door shut. Fred was trapped inside a cave. Then he heard a voice. 'Find the key to freedom and the doors will open.'
Fred searched through many corridors, but found nothing. Eventually, he arrived at the final corridor. He opened a door and discovered a huge red-eyed owl.

Karl Egeland (9)
Plaxtol Primary School

Tiny Tales Fiction From Kent

Tom's Great Escape!

100 foot tall, brick barbed wire wall stands in front of me, the gate to freedom. There's no turning back now, the prison guards are coming. This is my one chance to be free! One, two, three, over I go.
Yes I've made it! I'm safe! Freedom here I come!

Grace Elliott (10)
St Mary's Catholic Primary School, Gillingham

A Muddy Entrance

I couldn't get out. My feet were trapped in the mud. Slowly my head went under. I fell to the ground. I looked around, attentively. I saw a boy talking to a weird being. A ray hit him and he fell to the ground, dead.
It was all a dream!

Elena Margerison (10)
St Mary's Catholic Primary School, Gillingham

War

She lay in bed dreaming about war. She could hear bombs being fired, people screaming, shouting and crying. She opened her curtains, she saw blood on the floor, people's wounds, people killing. She saw Mum on the floor. Was that Mum on the path? I wonder if she is alive?

Katie Lepore (10)
St Mary's Catholic Primary School, Gillingham

Baited Breath

He waited in the shadows. His breath quickened as he heard the soft, padded footsteps on the cold, hard floor. He decided to take the chance. He leapt from his hiding place. He waited with baited breath for the monster to come in the room.
In walked a ginger cat!

Samuel Atkins (10)
St Mary's Catholic Primary School, Gillingham

Three Old Friends

Harry, Hermione and Ron were making a potion that would make them fly. They started mixing it.

Hermione said, 'This is going to be a great potion.' She poured it out and tasted it. Suddenly with a puff they had turned old. They were wrinkly, smelly and very ugly.

Gemma Maxey (10)
St Mary's Catholic Primary School, Gillingham

Help!

'They're coming Doctor,' I shouted. He went into the TARDIS, the monster almost got me. It hurt me by the tip of its teeth. I fell, I screamed, the pain was unbearable. My leg was burning. I found the strength to get up and go into the TARDIS. It started.

Jade O'Connell (10)
St Mary's Catholic Primary School, Gillingham

Is It A Flying Fish?

Plunge the pet goldfish did a somersault in the air. 'Augh fish fingers,' he landed back in the dirty bowl. He wanted to escape then he bounced off the rock! Up, up and away. Plunge flew out the bowl.

'Wee!' the fish screamed, but then he landed in the bin.

Macauly McKenzie (10)
St Mary's Catholic Primary School, Gillingham

The Truck

There I lay silently gasping for air, I was totally paralysed. I was trying to move but I was distracted by the roar of a black monster truck, one of the deadliest cars in the world. As if out of nowhere the black truck reversed. Horror! 'Is this the end?'

Rochelle Garcia (10)
St Mary's Catholic Primary School, Gillingham

Tiny Tales Fiction From Kent

Princess Mirror Bell

There it was. A normal mirror, plain, silver, standing on the dressing table.
Sophie was in the bedroom, when out of nowhere she heard a voice whispering, 'Come closer to it.'
She went to it, it had a palace in the background with a twin like her called Mirrobell.

Phoebe Vadgama (10)
St Mary's Catholic Primary School, Gillingham

Is It A Ghost?

I lay silently in my bed, twisting and turning, trying to get to sleep. I heard a creak on the landing. It got louder and louder. I hid under the covers, I was absolutely petrified. All I wanted was Mum by my side. Suddenly the door swung open. I screamed.

Molly Weller (9)
St Mary's Catholic Primary School, Gillingham

Tiny Tales Fiction From Kent

Freedom!

I was lying by the huge steel door, waiting for the special moment to get out. My wicked stepmum opened the door to check up on me, she didn't say a word just stared at my big blue eyes. I barged past.
'I'm free! After ten years I'm free!'

Katie Rayner (10)
St Mary's Catholic Primary School, Gillingham

I Wasn't Alone

I was looking round when I realised I wasn't alone. I stopped and listened. I heard some footsteps getting louder and louder. It suddenly got cold, really cold. I froze with fear. I opened my mouth to yell *help!* but nothing came out. I slowly turned myself round and … *Help!*

Claire Scholes (10)
St Mary's Catholic Primary School, Gillingham

Tiny Tales Fiction From Kent

The Bats In The Belfry

I pulled the rope for the belfry wondering what would happen. The bats from the belfry scattered all over the room and suddenly a huge trapdoor flung open. I climbed down there, it led to a secret hidden cave with dozens of hidden treasures. It just had to be Heaven!

Monica Chapinduka (10)
St Mary's Catholic Primary School, Gillingham

The Moonlight Shadow Creeper

The footsteps came in the direction of the moonlit room. She searched for a shadow to hide in. Louise found one, right in between the wardrobe and the bed. It would be a tight squeeze. Louise's blue eyes scanned the man who entered the room. He turned, she was discovered!

Shannon Rudden (10)
St Mary's Catholic Primary School, Gillingham

Aliens In My House

I don't know how I got there. I was at the cellar stairs. Downstairs I could hear some kind of strange language. I could see something green. I automatically walked down the stairs. Green monsters stared up at me.
Suddenly I woke up and something green was by the door.

William Brittain (10)
St Mary's Catholic Primary School, Gillingham

Hand In The Seas

I've been lost at sea for fifteen minutes. I'm drifting slowly along the water. The current's pulling me down. The waves are smooth but I fear they will get high. I screech, some sort of thing is pulling me down. I glance down, what could it be? It's a hand.

Shamyla Jahangiri (10)
St Mary's Catholic Primary School, Gillingham

Tiny Tales Fiction From Kent

The Nightmare

I was in the forest, then a dark figure appeared. I started running then I tripped. I shut my eyes tight. I opened them and the dark figure was about to hurt me. *Argh ...*
I woke up safely in bed. What a nightmare! I wonder what I'll dream next.

Rachel Sutton (10)
St Paul's CE Primary School, Swanley Village

Alien Attack

Help, help, aliens are attacking. Police come quickly please. Wait there are no policemen, everybody has died. I'm the only person left. 'Destroy all humans that are alive,' they keep saying. The aliens come closer. 'Destroy the human, destroy.'
Aarrgh …!
Oh, it was just a dream.

Jack Gilbert (11)
St Paul's CE Primary School, Swanley Village

My Birthday Surprise

I woke up to find my dad getting ready for work with a big smile on his face. He was the first one to say happy birthday to me. He gave me a big cuddle. I went into the lounge and saw my presents. It was a big bunch, yay!

Catherine Ashley-Smith (10)
St Paul's CE Primary School, Swanley Village

The Mystery Smoke

A cloud of pink smoke rose into the air. I could not breathe. If I did not get oxygen soon I would fall unconscious. I started to get sleepy, my eyes started to close …

'Nicola, wake up, I asked you to do your twelve times table.'

Oops, I'm in trouble!

Nicola Freeman (10)
St Paul's CE Primary School, Swanley Village

Tiny Tales Fiction From Kent

Untitled

It was a dark and stormy night, lighting echoed in the big dark cave. I noticed a big hairy ape in the corner, then it got up and was getting closer and closer! Then I heard my little brother Tyler waking me up.
It was all just a dream.

Ryan Russell (11)
St Paul's CE Primary School, Swanley Village

The Haunted Castle

I was dared by my friends to enter the haunted castle. When I entered I heard and smelt dripping pungent water. I felt uneasy as I heard a loud creaking noise. I heard it come from the door to the left. I went in and felt a hand grab me!

James Green (11)
St Paul's CE Primary School, Swanley Village

The Ghost Of Charles Darwin

We got off the coach, and went inside. *Crash! Bang! Wallop!* We heard a strange sound coming from one of the rooms. Me, Paige, Molly and Beth ran as fast as we could to find the ghost of Charles Darwin was there standing behind the door.

'Mrs Milan,' we screamed.

Emmie Cason (11)
St Paul's CE Primary School, Swanley Village

In The Deep Dark Wood

It was a cold winter's night and I decided to go for a walk in the woods. It was a really spooky wood, and I could hear lots of strange noises. I saw a fox that was eating a rabbit.
I woke up and realised it was a bad dream.

Sam Cason (10)
St Paul's CE Primary School, Swanley Village

The Sound Of Music Auditions

'Next! Honestly hasn't anybody got talent? Time for tea break … Now that's over, someone impress me! Next. 1, 2, 3, go!'
'The hills are alive.'
'You're amazing! You're hired …! But do the job.'
It was good to be true.
'Don't worry, just think of your favourite things … like me!'

Thea Medland (10)
St Paul's CE Primary School, Swanley Village

An Alien Visting Earth

One day I saw a spaceship over me, it was black. It started shooting the city with red lasers. Then it started shooting me. I ran and ran, then I realised that it only shot when people ran and then I spotted Dad who was holding a model spaceship.

Nicholas Couvret (10)
St Paul's CE Primary School, Swanley Village

Fairy Land

One day in the woods I saw a fairy then more. They were very pretty and delicate. They used to share their secrets and tell me everything. They would come to my house and play with me. We used to play teachers.
'Melina, wake up.'
It was just a dream.

Melina Tomas (10)
St Paul's CE Primary School, Swanley Village

The End Of The World

As the sky grew dark, most of the world was plunged into darkness. The world held its breath waiting for one of the greatest impacts it had ever seen. Most of the world's inhabitants already knew there was no way of escaping this fate. Sadly most wouldn't survive.

Carl Aylett (11)
St Paul's CE Primary School, Swanley Village

A Nice Surprise

There they were. Just standing in the corridor, staring and waiting for me to move. My spine tingled up to my neck, not knowing what they were going to do next! Then suddenly they pounced on me like a tiger.
I realised it was only my pet kittens.

Alice Spinola (11)
St Paul's CE Primary School, Swanley Village

I Hate Custard!

Voodoo's shadow covered James. A trembling bony hand stretched out. Without thinking twice Voodoo jabbed a dose of special anaesthetic into James. Back at Voodoo's Surgeries all was still but James, hanging above a giant vat of custard! Screaming and wriggling! Suddenly James fell. 'Noooo!' he shouted, waking himself up.

Thomas Franklin (10)
St Paul's CE Primary School, Swanley Village

Going Bananas

We were asleep in bed late at night. We heard an almighty *bang!* Suddenly everybody sleeping in the house awoke and turned the lights on. We gathered in the living room to discuss what the noise was that startled us. We found the bananas had fallen off the sideboard.

Harry Gilbert (10)
St Paul's CE Primary School, Swanley Village

The Big Bang

The *big bang. Thump, thump, thump,* I heard coming up the stairs. *Bang!* Opened the door. I jumped halfway across my room.
'Do you want some milk and chocolate chip biscuits?' Mum said.
'Oh! Mum! You scared the life out of me! Yes I would, thank you Mum.'

Charlotte Summers (9)
St Paul's CE Primary School, Swanley Village

Tiny Tales Fiction From Kent

The Great Goal

Yes, this is the chance I've been waiting for. Cross it in now, I'm not marked. Here it comes, don't let the defender clear the ball. He's missed it, he didn't jump high enough to head it! There it goes on its way to the top corner! What a goal!

David Mason (10)
St Paul's CE Primary School, Swanley Village

Sydney's Birthday

One day Sydney woke up and it was her birthday. She went downstairs and opened her presents. Sydney opened one and it was a sparkly dress for tonight because she was having a party. She got in her dress and went to the party and was very, very excited.

Libby Vinten (9)
St Peter Chanel RC Primary School, Sidcup

The Spirit

Silent. The spirit lay waiting for its prey to come a bit too close to its resting ground. Someone went up to the graveyard. The spirit sensed him and attacked.

The next day the world was all missing a number of their family. The spirit had finally got them all!

Toby Sanford (9)
St Peter Chanel RC Primary School, Sidcup

Untitled

Oh no, the terrifying sprint race! I wish I hadn't come to school today. We lined up, my tummy started to churn, I was shivering.
'Ready, steady, go!' shouted our teacher. I ran for my life, after a couple of seconds I realised that I was in the lead! First!

Holly Dixon (9)
St Peter Chanel RC Primary School, Sidcup

The Rainbow

One day a little girl named Lea saw a rainbow and decided to follow it. On her way she saw an owl. The owl told her to go no further but she did not listen. She walked on.
Suddenly everybody watching clapped. The best school play ever. Then Lea bowed.

Jade Verrico (9)
St Peter Chanel RC Primary School, Sidcup

The Castle

The deep black ocean under the creaky bridge howling like a cat, the prisoner getting out. Inside the castle, red velvet and dim light, working my way round, steep staircase, mouldy floor. Suddenly I heard a scream, a black cat. *Argh!* I screamed, the cat got me. Suddenly I awoke.

Rebecca Harvey (9)
St Peter Chanel RC Primary School, Sidcup

My Dream

I got caught in a whirlwind and landed in cartoon land. All my favourite characters were there. A goblin came along and tried to take the king and queen, I had magic powers and stopped him …
Then Mum woke me up.

Jade Hutchinson (9)
St Peter Chanel RC Primary School, Sidcup

The Deep Forest Of Wolves

There is a deep forest behind the camping site where the boy went camping. He was playing hide-and-seek with his family in the forest. Suddenly there was a howl in the distance, the boy hid. The wolf saw him and the boy was never seen again.

Reece Wright (10)
St Peter Chanel RC Primary School, Sidcup

The Haunted School

Hi I'm Tom. My school is freaky. Tonight I am going to check what it's like at night-time. It's night, so I'm going in. I hear a noise. I'd better go and see what it is. Wait a minute, that's a ghost! *Argh!* What a terrifying school.

Thomas Monaghan (10)
St Peter Chanel RC Primary School, Sidcup

On My Bike

It was my first time on my bike without stabilisers. I was excited and scared. My dad helped me to push off. It was a very hard push. I went wonky at first, then I fell down … down. I never want to go on a bike again!

Ela Kutereba (7)
St Peter Chanel RC Primary School, Sidcup

Sparkle In The Woods

One day Sparkle, the fairy, was flying through the fresh air to pick some flowers. Suddenly a big grizzly monster jumped out from a tree in front of her.

Argh! She screamed and fell. He came up to see if she was okay … It was only a dream.

Caitlin Wyatt (8)
St Peter Chanel RC Primary School, Sidcup

A Couple Of Fairies And A Monster

In Fairy World there was a terrible threat. The monster was about. Once, Rose the fairy met Thorn the elf, they wanted to defeat the monster. So they climbed up the spooky mountain and found him, he was waiting for his tea! The couple happily scared away the big monster.

Olivia Douglas (7)
St Peter Chanel RC Primary School, Sidcup

Tiny Tales Fiction From Kent

The Maze

On a sizzling day, a silly girl called Sophie went into a maze. Her heart thumped like feet walking. See how silly she was? She was only three steps away from the door - out!

Sophie Young (8)
St Peter Chanel RC Primary School, Sidcup

We Won The Lottery

While eating my breakfast the radio called out this week's lottery winners. We all jumped out of our chairs when the radio called out our numbers! The doorbell rang. I opened the door, there stood a man holding a £10,000 cheque!

Isabella Coleman (8)
St Peter Chanel RC Primary School, Sidcup

Jumping On My Bed

I was towering way up high, trembling left to right. Going to drop … going to … oh no, *Argh!* Oh no, what shall I do? I'm going to … *Argh!* Oh yes I am on my bed. It was a dream.

Louise Rumble (8)
St Peter Chanel RC Primary School, Sidcup

The Cry For Help

One day there was an old man. He was baking some bread in his kitchen when he heard cries for help. He looked upstairs and down and all around, but could not find where the noise was coming from.
After hours of looking he finally realised it was the radio.

Francesca Hart (7)
St Peter Chanel RC Primary School, Sidcup

Ladybird And Bee

There once was a ladybird who sat in a tree and there was a buzz of a bee. The bee saw Ladybird and Ladybird saw Bee. They sat with a plop and Mother, called Mop, went to shop, Ladybird and Bee made a friend and that was the end.

Santini Holmes (6)
St Peter Chanel RC Primary School, Sidcup

Barney's Magic Glasses

Barney needed glasses. He went with his mum to the opticians. When he tried on his new glasses, he was amazed. He saw a magical world full of huge, scary dinosaurs.
'How do your new glasses feel Barney?'
'Really brilliant Mum. I wish I had got new glasses ages ago!'

Erin Ferris (7)
St Peter Chanel RC Primary School, Sidcup

The Magical Mermaid And Me

I was swimming in the deep blue ocean. I realised a mermaid was swimming with me. She told me to follow her. I did. She led me to a magical place. I felt sand on my skin. I was buried in the sand … it had all been a dream.

Victoria O'Neill (7)
St Peter Chanel RC Primary School, Sidcup

The Mystery Dream

A nice sunny day, spring was here. Suddenly a wolf jumped out, it was alright until blackness was everywhere. Crumbling rocks under me. I woke up, it was all a daydream, although it seemed real. My mum yelled, I'd dropped the cup.

Jerome Swan (8)
St Simon of England RC (VA) Primary School, Ashford

Tiny Tales Fiction From Kent

The Creature Costume

Last night I was watching a movie. Suddenly I heard a thunderstorm. I was going to scare my sister but a big creature jumped up and roared. I ran to my room, I heard my sister laughing. I peeked and saw my sister taking off the creature costume.

Ewen Rai (8)
St Simon of England RC (VA) Primary School, Ashford

The Monster

One day I walked down the street. After, I went through the play area. A big monster jumped out from under a prickly bush. It roared, the sound was a big, fierce, screaming sound. I was really scared.
Suddenly it was silent, the monster was gone.

Harry Dryland (7)
St Simon of England RC (VA) Primary School, Ashford

Tiny Tales Fiction From Kent

The Alien

One day I was in my garden and then I saw an alien, it had a gun!
I ran! I was slow and I locked the door. It started to rain. The alien was really my brother with a water pistol! So I let him in.

Ben Fraser (8)
St Simon of England RC (VA) Primary School, Ashford

The Monster

Bill went to the forest and found a massive footprint, he thought it was a monster print, but was it? Bill told his mum but she didn't believe him. So they went to the woods and they were eaten.

Three days later people found the bones on the ground.

Max May (8)
St Simon of England RC (VA) Primary School, Ashford

Tiny Tales Fiction From Kent

The Breakdown

I went on a train at 8.30 on Monday night …
Suddenly the train broke down. My friend John was seated on the train. John fell over and hit his head. John's head was cracked open. Tom was shouting.
Finally the train started working and we had a nice holiday.

Luke Brooke (8)
St Simon of England RC (VA) Primary School, Ashford

The Trick Went Wrong

Doughine, a magician, and his best friend Sally, the mad scientist, would come up with the most clever tricks. One day Sally's experiment went wrong. Sally accidentally picked up crows' feet instead of frogs' feet, the room filled with smoke. Sally turned into a caveman, Doughine turned into a dinosaur.

Megan Fisher (8)
St Simon of England RC (VA) Primary School, Ashford

Tiny Tales Fiction From Kent

The Big Storm

I was in bed when a storm started. All of a sudden a crash of lightning came in the room. There was a Bratz doll. I took it to school and I came home with it. I put it by my bed and in the morning it wasn't there.

Emma Knight (8)
St Simon of England RC (VA) Primary School, Ashford

The Mystery

One sunny day Chloe was walking in the dark woods. She fell over, it was a footprint in the woods. She followed the footprints. She saw a bit of white fur on a branch.
Her mum shouted, 'Come on Chloe, come back home.'
Was there a monster?

Claudia Knight (8)
St Simon of England RC (VA) Primary School, Ashford

Tiny Tales Fiction From Kent

Never Saw Again

One day Rachel was walking by the sea, when she saw a boat, she went over to it and got in. Then the engine started. 'Oh no,' she said. She got into the middle of the ocean. Then Rachel disappeared, Rachel was never seen again. Do you think she survived?

Hannah Peirson (8)
St Simon of England RC (VA) Primary School, Ashford

When Ronija Walked Outside

When Ronija woke up she went outside.
Mum asked, 'Where are you going?'
'I'm going for a walk,' shouted Ronija.
She walked and walked, then she stopped. She saw some footprints and saw something white behind the footprints. I think it is an abominable snowman.
Will she escape?

Inithaa Mariyanayagam (7)
St Simon of England RC (VA) Primary School, Ashford

Tiny Tales Fiction From Kent

The Little Girl And Her Mother

There once was a girl, she whined to her mother that she wanted to go to a club. She wanted to go now. Her mother felt weird because she had never been before but her mum took her anyway. Then she silently felt good.

Shakira Griffin (8)
St Simon of England RC (VA) Primary School, Ashford

The Terrible Pencil Case

One stormy night, I was watching the lightning, when lightning shot onto the garden shed. I went out and I saw a pencil case. I took it to school every day but it got me into trouble. So the next day I threw it into the bin.

Jack Macdonald (8)
St Simon of England RC (VA) Primary School, Ashford

Tiny Tales Fiction From Kent

Joe's Injury

Joe had a job, the job was a footballer, until he got injured, so he could not play.
One day he went to his old football coach and grumbled, 'Why can't I play anymore?'
'You can,' he shouted.
'Thank you coach,' replied Joe, and he danced in happiness.

Georgia Belfiore (8)
St Simon of England RC (VA) Primary School, Ashford

The Magnificent Tunnel

One scary dark night it was pouring with rain, thunder and lightning. I went outside, I was so scared and suddenly I fell down a dark, dark hole. The hole was so big that I couldn't climb out so I dug a tunnel, crawled out and hurried back home.

Isabelle Lugg (8)
St Simon of England RC (VA) Primary School, Ashford

Tiny Tales Fiction From Kent

The Holiday

Sally went on holiday and stayed in a fancy hotel. She saw some water leading to the swimming pool. She followed it and she thought she saw a Loch Ness monster. It was time to go home. Even now she does not know if there was a Loch Ness monster.

Monica Jarvis (8)
St Simon of England RC (VA) Primary School, Ashford

Thunder

When I saw the thunder last night, I was scared. I was looking out of the window with sadness on my face. No play! No chatting! No anything! I thought sadly. Mum came downstairs, gave me a hug but still my face was sad. I went to bed.

Tazmyn Burgess (8)
St Simon of England RC (VA) Primary School, Ashford

Tiny Tales Fiction From Kent

The Ghost

I went to have a bath and pink goo came out of the tap. The pink attacked me. It took me to a cave. I got very scared, so I got out my spray. It turned him into a ghost. I sprayed my body spray again and the ghost died.

Aimee Robinson (8)
St Simon of England RC (VA) Primary School, Ashford

Bermuda Triangle

One day a captain called Bill was on the Mary Rose. His crew were sailing but then they sailed into the Bermuda Triangle, and they were never seen again. Nobody has solved the mystery so if you sail on the sea be careful all the time!

Sally Hazelwood (8)
St Simon of England RC (VA) Primary School, Ashford

The Mysterious Triangle

One stormy night a boat to New York accidentally went into the Bermuda Triangle in the sea. It disappeared into thin air, no one knows what happened, including the captain, Sticky Beard. They found the spot and closed it forever and ever. Everyone can go out to sea again.

Scott Dorman (8)
St Simon of England RC (VA) Primary School, Ashford

The Alien

A meteor crashed in my garden. My dad looked at what it was. It was an alien egg! I brought the egg to school. The egg hatched and then the alien heads blew up. The mum and dad alien came back and picked the heads up.
We all went home.

Ben Pali (7)
St Simon of England RC (VA) Primary School, Ashford

A Thunderstorm

Last night I watched Shrek the movie. Suddenly I heard a thunderstorm, then there was a shadow, but it was only my big brother. Next I saw my front room go all light when I'd already turned the lights off and then I knew it was the thunderstorm.

Danielle Rice (8)
St Simon of England RC (VA) Primary School, Ashford

Roller Coaster

I was trembling! My roller coaster experience was beginning. My white knuckles gripped the rail tightly and it moved. It went in every direction, left, right, upside down and accelerated extremely fast. Then it stopped with a jolt. I opened my eyes, I sighed in relief as the ride ended.

Nicholas Pearce (10)
St Stephen's Junior School, Canterbury

Rescue?

We've been walking five days now, my throat is dry. Our water supply ran out yesterday. I keep seeing tranquil oases of never-ending water. Will the smoke signal we sent last night work? Then my friends start shouting, and I see a helicopter.
We are safe!

Gwendy Grynfeld (11)
St Stephen's Junior School, Canterbury

My Loved One

That day it happened, the tragedy of my whole life. The day I lost my loved one. I'd give life itself to see her again. Through the woods she led me, her big brown eyes gazed at me. Later that night a lost memory that tore my heart away.

Grace Davis (11)
St Stephen's Junior School, Canterbury

I Wish I Hadn't

I wish I hadn't done what I did on that cold Wednesday night. Wednesday hadn't always been a good day, Mum usually forgot to help me with my homework or my school contribution fund. We were fine, until that happened. I'd started the fight with my parents. Divorce is horrible!

Jasmin Brown (10)
St Stephen's Junior School, Canterbury

Information

We hope you have enjoyed reading this book - and that you will continue to enjoy it in the coming years.

If you like reading and writing, drop us a line or give us a call and we'll send you a free information pack. Alternatively visit our website at www.youngwriters.co.uk

Write to:
Young Writers Information,
Remus House,
Coltsfoot Drive,
Peterborough,
PE2 9JX
Tel: (01733) 890066
Email: youngwriters@forwardpress.co.uk